A Note to Parents and Caregivers:

Read-it! Readers are for children who are just starting on the amazing road to reading. These beautiful books support both the acquisition of reading skills and the love of books.

The PURPLE LEVEL presents basic topics and objects using high frequency words and simple language patterns.

The RED LEVEL presents familiar topics using common words and repeating sentence patterns.

The BLUE LEVEL presents new ideas using a larger vocabulary and varied sentence structure.

The YELLOW LEVEL presents more challenging ideas, a broad vocabulary, and wide variety in sentence structure.

The GREEN LEVEL presents more complex ideas, an extended vocabulary range, and expanded language structures.

The ORANGE LEVEL presents a wide range of ideas and concepts using challenging vocabulary and complex language structures.

When sharing a book with your child, read in short stretches, pausing often to talk about the pictures. Have your child turn the pages and point to the pictures and familiar words. And be sure to reread favorite stories or parts of stories.

There is no right or wrong way to share books with children. Find time to read with your child, and pass on the legacy of literacy.

Adria F. Klein, Ph.D.
Professor Emeritus
California State University
San Bernardino, California

Managing Editor: Bob Temple
Creative Director: Terri Foley
Editor: Peggy Henrikson
Editorial Adviser: Andrea Cascardi
Copy Editor: Laurie Kahn
Designer: Nathan Gassman
Page production: Picture Window Books
The illustrations in this book were rendered with watercolor.

Picture Window Books
5115 Excelsior Boulevard
Suite 232
Minneapolis, MN 55416
1-877-845-8392
www.picturewindowbooks.com

Printed in the United States of America.

All books published by Picture Window Books
are manufactured with paper containing at least
10 percent post-consumer waste.

Library of Congress Cataloging-in-Publication Data
Blackaby, Susan.
Steadfast tin soldier / by Hans Christian Andersen ; adapted by
Susan Blackaby ; illustrated by Charlene DeLage.
p. cm. — (Read-it! readers fairy tales)
Summary: The perilous adventure of a toy soldier who loves a
paper dancing girl culminates in tragedy for both of them.
ISBN 978-1-4048-0226-1 (hardcover)
ISBN 978-1-4048-0476-0 (paperback)
[1. Fairy tales. 2. Toys—Fiction.] I. DeLage, Charlene, 1944– ill.
II. Andersen, H. C. (Hans Christian), 1805–1875. Standhaftige
tinsoldat. English. III. Title. IV. Series.
PZ8.B5595 St 2004
[E]—dc21
                                                    2003006113

The Steadfast Tin Soldier

by Hans Christian Andersen

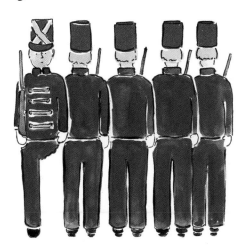

Adapted by Susan Blackaby

Illustrated by Charlene DeLage

Reading Advisers:
Adria F. Klein, Ph.D.
Professor Emeritus, California State University
San Bernardino, California

Kathy Baxter, M.A.
Former Coordinator of Children's Services
Anoka County (Minnesota) Library

Susan Kesselring, M.A.
Literacy Educator
Rosemount-Apple Valley-Eagan (Minnesota) School District

PiCTURE WiNDOW BOOKS
Minneapolis, Minnesota

A boy once had a set of tin soldiers.
All 25 of them were brothers.
They were made out of the same
tin spoon.

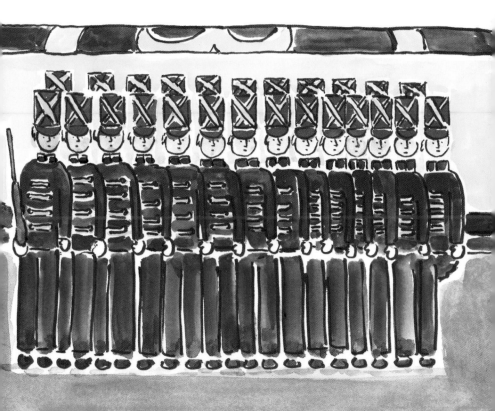

All of the soldiers were exactly alike except the last one. He had only one leg. But he stood as steadfast on one leg as the others did on two.

The tin soldiers stood on a table covered with toys. The best toy was a paper castle. Wax swans swam on a glass pool in front of it.

A tiny paper dancer stood at the
castle door. She was dressed like
a princess. She wore a blue ribbon
scarf held by a tinsel rose.

The dancer kicked one leg up high behind her. The tin soldier couldn't see it. He thought she had only one leg, too.

"She is the wife for me," he thought.
"But she lives in a fine castle!
My brothers and I live in our box
like sardines
in a can."

Still, the tin soldier wanted to meet the dancer. He stretched out behind a box on the table where he could see her.

That night the toys had fun while the family slept. The chalk doodled on the slate. The nutcrackers played tag. The tin soldiers rattled their box top.

The racket woke the canary.
Tweet! Tweet! The bird sang.
In the hubbub, the tin soldier
stayed hidden. He watched
the dancer as she stood on tiptoe.

Bong! Bong! The clock chimed.
At midnight on the dot, the box
on the table flipped its lid.
Out popped Jack-in-the-box.

"Don't wish for what you can't have, soldier!" yelled Jack. The tin soldier ignored him. "Just you wait!" cried Jack.

In the morning, the boy set the tin soldier by an open window. All of a sudden, he toppled out! Did the wind blow him, or was it Jack?

16

The boy spent hours looking.
He didn't see the soldier stuck
between two stones. It started raining,
and the boy went inside.

After the storm, two boys spotted
the soldier's leg sticking up.
"Look what I found!" said one.
"He needs a boat," said the other.

The boys sent the tin soldier down the gutter in a paper boat.
The boat bobbed and swirled into a dark tunnel under a bridge.

"Now where am I?" wondered the tin soldier. "This must be one of Jack's tricks. I wish the dancer were here with me right now."

Just then a big rat appeared.

"Stop and pay the toll!" he snapped.

The tin soldier sailed swiftly by.

The tin soldier held his head high.
He didn't even flinch as the boat
rushed on. Water crashed
and splashed all around him.

The boat filled with water. Sadly, the soldier thought of the dancer. "Farewell, soldier, brave and true," he said to himself. "Now there's nothing to save you."

The paper boat fell apart. Dark water closed over the tin soldier's head. Then a big fish came along and swallowed him. *Gulp!*

The fish wiggled and swam.
Then he was still for a long time.
"What next?" wondered the tin
soldier. Suddenly, he saw light.

"Look!" said the cook. "The fish had a tin soldier in his tummy!" She brought the soldier to the dinner table

for everyone to see.

The tin soldier was thrilled. He was
right back where he started!
There were his brothers. There was
the dancer he loved, still on tiptoe!

Then, for no reason, the boy grabbed the soldier and threw him into the fire! Jack must have made him do it!

The flames were as hot as the love
in the tin soldier's heart. He began
to melt. But still he stood tall, looking
up at the dancer.

Then a gust of wind blew the dancer
into the fire. She burst into a quick
flame and was gone. The soldier
melted into a lump.

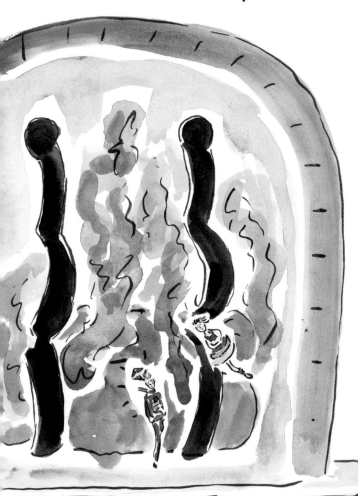

The next day, the cook cleaned out the fireplace. In the ashes, she found a little tin heart and a tinsel rose burned black as coal.

More *Read-it!* Readers

Bright pictures and fun stories help you practice your reading skills. Look for more books at your level.

Beauty and the Beast
Brave Little Tailor, The
Bremen Town Musicians, The
Fisherman and His Wife, The
Frog Prince, The
Hansel and Gretel
Little Mermaid, The
Princess and the Pea, The
Puss in Boots
Rapunzel
Rumpelstiltskin
Shoemaker and His Elves, The

On the Web

FactHound offers a safe, fun way to find Web sites related to topics in this book. All of the sites on FactHound have been researched by our staff.

1. Visit *www.facthound.com*
2. Type in this special code:
   1404802266
3. Click on the FETCH IT button.

Your trusty FactHound will fetch the best sites for you! A complete list of *Read-it!* Readers is available on our Web site:
www.picturewindowbooks.com